Printed in England. Ref. 570 SBN 85503000 4

When the mice started to whisper about 'STUFFING' Buffie, the teddy bear with only one eye and holes in his paws, decided that he must get out of the attic.

He had been put away there when the little girl who owned him grew into a big girl who did not want to play with teddy bears any more.

So in the attic he stayed day after day, and month after month, until everybody had forgotten Buffie except the mice.

He had been fond of them for he was very lonely, until the day when Mr. Mouse came up to him boldly and squeaked,

"Mother says could you spare a bit of your stuffing for our nest?"

Then Buffie scowled and growled quite fiercely, and shook his head so hard that the cobweb between his ears fell off.

Then the bear shook himself for he was very dusty, and did a few exercises, for he was very stiff after not being played with for such a long time.

"Those mice will nibble a hole in my middle and steal my stuffing when I am asleep," he thought, and prowled all round the attic looking for a way of escape.

The trapdoor in the floor was bolted, there was no window, and only a small skylight in the low roof.

Buffie found a little child's old umbrella among the odds and ends piled in the corner, and used it to push the skylight open, for the thought of losing his stuffing had made him both clever and adventurous.

Then he hooked the handle on the edge and climbed up and out on to the roof, much to the surprise of a family of starlings who sat there gossiping.

Next moment the little bear was rolling and bumping over the tiles sloping so steeply to the edge.

Luckily the starlings came to his rescue, and caught hold of him just in time to stop his wild career into space.

After thanking them Buffie climbed up and collected his umbrella, then he sat on the tiles and looked down; it was a very long way to the ground.

Buffie opened the umbrella, shut his one eye tight and jumped.

The umbrella acted as a parachute and he floated down quite gently, landing in the garden of the house next door.

The little bear looked up at a window which had bars on it, and through them three furry faces were watching him.

They belonged to three Teddy Bears.

The biggest bear pushed open the window,

"I am Tough Bear," he growled in a very gruff voice, "and this is Tinkle Bear, because she hums a tune instead of growling."

"And *I* am Tiny Bear," said the little one in a very squeaky voice."

Buffie told them his name and explained that his owner had forgotten all about him.

"May I play with you?" he asked politely.

The three bears climbed out of the window and slid down a drainpipe, they shook paws with Buffie and Tough Bear growled,

"The children have gone to the sea today and left us behind, so we are going to have a holiday too and you may join us if you like."

"We have a kettle and a mug, buns in a paper bag, and a box of matches in Tough Bear's trouser pocket," said Tinkle Bear in her tinkling voice.

"We are going to camp in the wood all day, Hurray! Hurray!" squeaked Tiny Bear getting quite excited.

So they set off with Tough Bear leading the way.

"We'll be Wild Bears," he growled as the others followed him, across the buttercup field, over the stepping stones of the little stream, and round the great tree trunks into the wood.

Buffie opened his umbrella and stuck the handle in the ground, then Tough Bear and Tinkle Bear hung their clothes round it to make a tent, because Wild Bears only wear fur coats.

Tiny Bear cried because *his* clothes were sewn on.

Then Buffie and Tough Bear went hunting and tracked down something which looked like a scrubbing brush, until it uncurled itself and scuttled away.

After that they climbed trees and swung on the branches; Tiny Bear fell off when an owl popped out of a hole to look at him.

Buffie found a store of nuts, but he did not know that they belonged to Mr. and Mrs. Grey Squirrel.

Tinkle Bear found two little wax pots of honey in a bumble bee's nest.

Tiny Bear found some wild strawberries.

Tough Bear gathered sticks and made a camp fire.

Tinkle Bear tied a leaf for a patch over Buffie's missing eye, then she hung the kettle over the fire and when it boiled they made elderflower tea.

There was a currant bun each, and just enough honey to attract a wasp and make the bears sticky.

They were wondering how to crack the nuts when—

there was an angry
scolding in the branches
above, followed by a
shower of fir cones; the
squirrels had discovered
the loss of their nuts.

Tough Bear and the
others crawled into their tent, and there they
stayed until the angry squirrels had collected
their nuts and gone away.

Then Buffie had a wonderful idea,

"I shall build a house in the tree top, and
never go back to the attic," he growled.

Tough Bear, Tinkle Bear, and Tiny Bear
soon helped him to build a little home
among the leaves and branches.

When it was finished they had to say
"Goodbye," put on their clothes, and go
home in time to welcome the children back
from the sea.

Buffie curled up in his tree top house and slept soundly until the birds wakened him with their morning song.

He was so happy in his new home all day until suddenly the wind started to blow hard; leaves rustled, branches waved wildly, and Buffie's home was blown out of the tree in a scatter of sticks.

The little bear had to hang on tight to a branch until the wind had passed.

Then he climbed to the top of the tree.

Down below he saw a strange sight; birds and animals were hurrying to the shelter of the wood, and in the distance, looming up against the sky was an ENORMOUS yellow dragon grubbing up great mouthfuls of earth in its jaws.

Grass, flowers, bushes, and the little homes among them, were fast disappearing as ground was cleared and ditches dug for a new road.

Buffie felt very sorry for the animals who were being chased away.

"I will *shoot* that dragon," he growled fiercely, scrambling down the tree trunk as fast

as he could, and wishing his umbrella was a gun.

The brave bear soon made a bow from a hazel sapling and the ribbon round his neck.

With a paw full of arrows made from sticks he marched out of the wood to shoot the dragon.

But as he got nearer the dragon seemed to grow bigger, and BIGGER, and BIGGER, and—how he roared and rumbled!

Hiding behind a foxglove Buffie aimed his bow straight at the great yellow monster.

Ping! went an arrow and Pong! Ping! went two more against his steel sides.

The dragon's head sank slowly to the ground and his roaring ceased.

"I have shot the dragon," growled

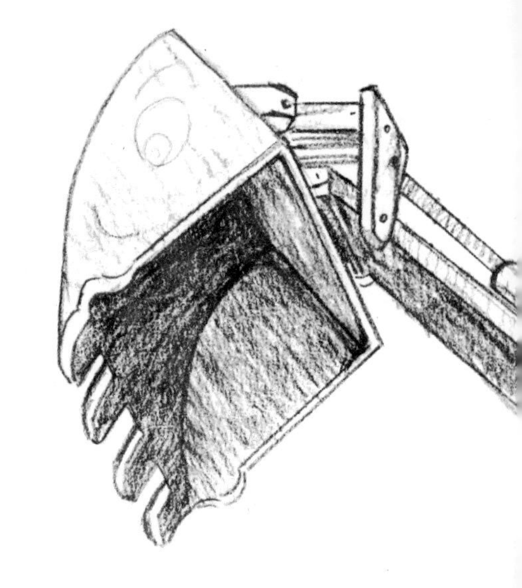

Buffie proudly, feeling very pleased with himself, but—he spoke too soon, for—you can never tell with dragons!

Up jerked the great yellow head again, the roarings and rumblings sounded louder than ever, and though the little bear shot all his remaining arrows, the dragon did not even seem to feel them, instead he suddenly lurched round and—CAME STRAIGHT AT BUFFIE! who dived into a nearby rabbit hole.

He crawled down a long dark passage, and came to a small cave at the end where four baby rabbits sat huddled together, listening to the rumbling noises overhead.

"You can't stay here," growled Buffie, "THE YELLOW DRAGON IS COMING! Run away as fast as you can."

But the bunnies were too frightened to move.

So the bear pushed them gently along the passage until they could run out and away to the safety of the wood.

But before he could follow

them huge jaws tore through the roof, and Buffie was scooped up with a mouthful of earth.

High in the air he went and then—BUMP! he landed on top of a lorry in a shower of earth and stones.

Luckily it was the last of the load and away went Buffie sitting on the big pile of earth.

As the lorry was driven through the wood branches brushed the top, and the little bear was caught up in them.

There he hung, unable to move, while the lorry rumbled on, and presently a boy and a girl came by and saw him.

They soon climbed the tree and released the little bear, then they took him home and their mother gave him a much needed bath.

When he was clean and dry she mended the holes in his paws, sewed on a twinkling button to replace his missing eye, and tied a new ribbon round his neck.

Now Buffie is a favourite toy with the children who will never forget finding a Wild Teddy Bear in the wood.

Sometimes he is taken with them for a picnic and meets Tough Bear, Tinkle Bear, and Tiny Bear again; they do not speak when the children are there but Buffie gives them a wink with his new twinkling button eye.

He never went back to look for his umbrella, so perhaps the woodland animals find it useful when going home from a party on a wet night.